The Little Griffin in the Acropolis Museum

The Little Griffin in the Acropolis Museum
Written by Mania Douka
Illustrated by Ino Karella
Cover design by George Pazalos
Translated by Dominique Sandis
Edited by Anna Knutson
Typography by Eleni Stavropoulou
Printed and bound in Greece

© Mania Douka, 2012
© PSICHOGIOS PUBLICATIONS S.A., Athens 2012

First edition: June 2012

ISBN 978-960-496-754-4

Psichogios Publications S.A. supports the Forest Stewardship Council (FSC®),
the leading international forest-certification organization.
Our books carrying the FSC label are printed on FSC®-certified paper.

ΕΚΔΟΣΕΙΣ ΨΥΧΟΓΙΟΣ Α.Ε.
Έδρα: Τατοΐου 121
144 52 Μεταμόρφωση
Βιβλιοπωλείο: Μαυρομιχάλη 1
106 79 Αθήνα
Τηλ.: 2102804800
Telefax: 2102819550
www.psichogios.gr
e-mail: info@psichogios.gr

PSICHOGIOS PUBLICATIONS S.A.
Head office: 121, Tatoiou Str.
144 52 Metamorfossi, Greece
Bookstore: 1, Mavromichali Str.
106 79 Athens, Greece
Tel.: 2102804800
Telefax: 2102819550
www.psichogios.gr
e-mail: info@psichogios.gr

MANIA DOUKA

The Little Griffin in the Acropolis Museum

Illustrated by Ino Karella

For Stefanos

Once upon a time there lived a little griffin with blue wings. He dwelled high above the Acropolis, his home. Every evening, the little griffin waited impatiently for the sun to go down. Then he would open his blue wings and fly free above the Holy Rock.

He would first fly to the Parthenon where he would meet the horsemen and their horses carved all around the temple. Then, inside the museum, he would wake up the statues and bring the beautiful paintings on the pottery urns to life. The little griffin would spend his time laughing, teasing and causing all kinds of mischief: that is, until the statues and urns were moved to the new Acropolis Museum and he had to bid goodbye to all his friends.

Without them, he was lonely and bored. One afternoon, he grew so upset that he began to cry, sobbing painfully.

The lion, perched high upon the roof of the holy temple, heard him and turned to ask:

"What's the matter, little griffin? Why do you cry?"

"My friends are gone..."

"But you can find your friends at the new Acropolis Museum."

"Oh?" said the little griffin. "Why didn't I think of that?"

He brushed his tears away hastily, waved goodbye to the lion and, opening his blue wings, flew to the new Acropolis Museum.

It was that time of day when the rays of the sun fall sideways onto the great glass window of the museum and give it a magical orange and golden hue. The little griffin slipped carefully through the closed doors and landed on the glass floor. Two clay statues of Nike stood at the entrance.

"What are you doing in the museum at this time of day, little griffin?" they asked.

"I've come to find my friends."

Both women whispered something between them and then said:

"You may enter. Good luck!"

The little griffin proceeded hurriedly across the upward sloping glass floor when he suddenly felt as if someone were watching him. Who could it be? He turned his head and caught sight of a forehead with two hazel eyes set into the niche of a pillar. Suddenly, the hazel eyes sparked and streams of light and color began to flow down onto the glass floor. Wherever they passed, green sprigs and vines sprang and spread, growing more and more until they merged together. Soon, little buds sprang, opening and transforming into bright multicolored flowers.

The little griffin stared captivated at the magical transformation before him. The new Acropolis Museum looked enchanted.

A beautiful dancer
began to sing, and
the gallery filled with
exquisite melodies.
"Come here, little
griffin," she called to him
in her musical voice.
"Come and dance with me."
The little griffin and
the dancer swirled and
twirled when suddenly,
a loud gushing noise
was heard.

Waves swelled, foamed, grew tall and then crashed onto the glass stairs. In the water, fighting with a man, was a sea creature. It was half-human and had a scaly fish tale.

The song and dance ended abruptly and three old men said in one voice:
"Little griffin, you mustn't disturb us at this hour when the mythical
Heracles is fighting with Triton, the son of Poseidon. You must return
to the Acropolis at once."

"Why must I go back?"

"Because I say so! I the three-bodied sea demon!"

"Three-bodied? But how is that possible?" wondered the little griffin.
Looking more closely, however, he saw that the sea demon had three
dragon-bodied figures and three human heads. Also, in each of its three
hands it held an article: fire, water, and a bird. The sight before him was
truly frightening and the little griffin didn't know what to do.

Right then the two hazel eyes appeared again.

"I need your help!" pleaded the little griffin.

"Here we are!" they replied and wrapped all three pairs of the demon's eyes in their flaming glance.

"I am ready to fight you," called out the demon, menacingly shaking the fiery brand he held in his hand.

Both opponents looked at each other. The invisible force of the two hazel eyes, however, was so strong that in the end, the three-bodied demon lowered all three of its heads. The brand fell from its first human hand and was extinguished in the water held by its second human hand, while the third hand opened and the bird flew away.

The three dragon-bodied figures
with their three intertwined serpentine
tails remained still.

"Pheww!" whispered the little griffin.
"I'd almost lost hope," he said and sighed
with relief.

In the next gallery, the little griffin was greeted by four white horses.

"Welcome!" they neighed cheerfully. "We know so many games we could play. Why don't you stay with us?"

"No!"

"And why not?"

"Because I'm looking for my friend, the little calf.
Have you seen him?"

"Just now!" replied two of them, nodding their
heads excitedly. The other two looked around
and then said:

"We haven't seen any calf."

"Oh!" said the little griffin, confused.

Two sphinxes, sitting on their marble columns, were watching the scene with much interest.

"Ha! It's obvious that the horses don't agree with each other!" they said with a smirk.

How strange sphinxes look with their human faces, thought the little griffin. They have the body of a lion but also have two huge eagle's wings on their backs.

"I'm not afraid of them," he said to himself and, plucking up his courage, he turned to them and asked: "Can you please help me find my friend the little calf?"

"Don't be so hasty, little griffin!" replied the first sphinx in a hoarse and hard voice.

"Do you like riddles?" asked the second, but before the little griffin could respond, she continued. "Here is a riddle you must solve."

Crystal are its walls
And the road is fraught with strife.
Four are its prisoners
With only one, the beast who guards.
Yet when they are released,
There, deftly hidden, you shall discover
The little calf about which you
so desperately wonder.

And with that, the sphinxes
became motionless on their marble
perches. Neither listened, neither
spoke. And the little griffin learned
nothing more from them again.

He thus went up to the wise old owl. Perhaps she would have something to tell him.

"Owl! Wise old owl!" he called.

The owl rotated her large round eyes once, then twice, and then she said:

"Hoohoo... hoohoo,"

"Could you please speak more clearly?" the little griffin asked politely. "Have you seen crystal walls anywhere? Do you know where I could find them?"

"Leave the owl alone and go away!" whistled the snake-guard, who stood menacingly opposite the owl, with its mouth wide open and its sharp teeth showing.

At that moment, a young woman nodded her head at him. A bright smile lit up her face and her long red hair fell onto her shoulders in waves.

The little griffin looked at her in wonder.

"You are so beautiful," he said.

The Peplophoros Kore smoothed her long robe with grace and then spoke in a sweet voice:

"I've heard that you are looking for your friend, the little calf. He's around here somewhere..."

"What do you suggest I should do?" asked the little griffin.

The young noblewoman was the one to give
the little griffin his reply.

"First of all, little griffin, you must do what
the two sphinxes asked you to do!"

"Yes, yes," agreed the other Korai, shaking
their heads cheerfully and making the ornate
gold earrings that decorated their ears
ring like little bells: ring, ring, ring.

When all became quiet again, the young
woman continued:

"The four prisoners are waiting for
you to release them!"

Then the little griffin, in a self-assured
voice, promised: "Nothing will make me
forget that! Nothing!"

"For the time being, however, the crystal walls are invisible to you," explained the Kore with almond-shaped eyes.

"Invisible?" repeated the little griffin with surprise.

"Yes," confirmed the Kore and continued enigmatically, "the horseman who rides the horse with the blue mane will help you understand."

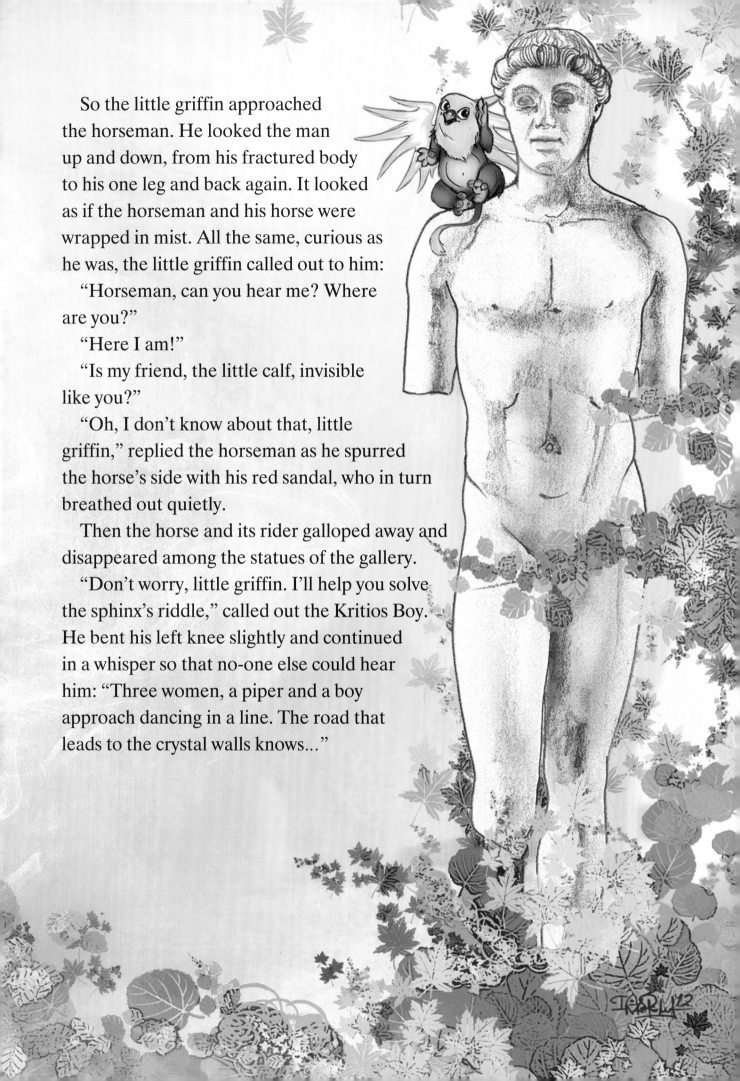

So the little griffin approached the horseman. He looked the man up and down, from his fractured body to his one leg and back again. It looked as if the horseman and his horse were wrapped in mist. All the same, curious as he was, the little griffin called out to him:

"Horseman, can you hear me? Where are you?"

"Here I am!"

"Is my friend, the little calf, invisible like you?"

"Oh, I don't know about that, little griffin," replied the horseman as he spurred the horse's side with his red sandal, who in turn breathed out quietly.

Then the horse and its rider galloped away and disappeared among the statues of the gallery.

"Don't worry, little griffin. I'll help you solve the sphinx's riddle," called out the Kritios Boy. He bent his left knee slightly and continued in a whisper so that no-one else could hear him: "Three women, a piper and a boy approach dancing in a line. The road that leads to the crystal walls knows..."

But before he could finish his words, the ground shook. Through the crack of light from a lightning bolt, the Goddess Athena appeared impressively before them.

"Did you reveal the secret?" the Goddess asked the youth, her eyes flashing with anger.

He shook his head with a silent "no".

"And you, Korai?" she asked again, looking around the room.

"No! No!" they too shook their heads, adorned with festive wreaths in her honor.

At that moment, the snakes that hung from the Goddess's aegis awoke chillingly, and the one she held in her hand rose and began to hiss.

"Sshhhh, ssshhh, silence!"

Obediently, the Kritios Boy and the Korai lowered their gaze and didn't speak again.

The little griffin repeated the Kritios Boy's words again and again as if it were a poem:

Three women, a piper and a boy.
Who can tell me where the road may be?

A deep echoing roar broke the silence. It was a lion's head.
"I'm not afraid!" he declared.
"Really? Are you telling the truth?"
The lion's head, tossing its thick mane from side to side, replied:

The little boy will tell you where the road may be.

A loud break and then a crack interrupted the lion's words.

"What's going on? What was that sound? Was it you?" asked the little griffin.

But the lion's head didn't respond.

The little griffin hesitantly held out his hand to pet the lion's mane, but immediately pulled it back in alarm. The mane was hard and frozen, like marble.

The lion's head had been turned into stone.

Strange music suddenly filled the room, first from afar, then from nearer by. A piper appeared, playing on his double pipe and followed by three women and a young boy. They held each other, hand in hand, dancing a cheerful dance.

"Do you like our dance, little griffin?" asked the first woman who had paused for a moment to catch her breath.

The second woman asked:

"Do you want to come with us?"

"I can't! I must solve the sphinx's riddle."

The third woman turned and looked at the young boy.

"Oh, I see," said the boy. "Little griffin, give me your hand."

The boy went to the front of the line and the rest of the dancers tagged along behind, following the rhythm of the music. At first the piper played a slow melody.

"Faster, faster!" called the little boy.

The rhythm of the music changed. It grew faster and faster.

"Faster, faster!" the boy continued to call.

And they went faster and faster and faster until at the end the little griffin realized that his feet weren't touching the floor anymore. With his eyes shut tightly, he began to turn and turn and turn.

The little griffin couldn't even begin to count how many times he had spun.
And when they finally stopped, he found himself alone, out of breath
and quite dizzy, holding tightly onto the piper's double pipe!

Before him stood the crystal walls that looked like a tightly closed glass
case. Inside he could make out its four prisoners: a rooster, a bull, a dog,
a bird and... oh... a sleeping lion.

The little griffin knocked on the window with the double pipe and
a narrow, brightly lit path appeared almost immediately, ending before
a large closed door.

"Open!" called out the little griffin.

The handle turned and the door opened! One after another, the four
prisoners slipped out of the case. Suddenly the lion rose, let out a terrifying
roar, and pounced.

"Who will save us now?" called out the rooster, the bull, the dog
and the bird in one unanimous voice.

"Me!" replied the little griffin.

He took a deep breath, mustered up all his courage and approached the lion who had already caught the rooster. He blew hard into the pipe and... a miracle happened!

A shower of golden sparks poured out the end. They wrapped around the glass case and the windows lit up so brightly that the lion, blinded by the glare, closed its eyes, opened its jaws, and the rooster escaped without a scratch.

"We're free!" called out the rooster, the bull, the dog and the bird, as they hurried away from the lion as fast as possible before the beast recovered.

"Hurray! Hurray!" called out the little griffin happily.

As the last golden sparks flickered sparingly, the little griffin wandered around the gallery.

"Little calf... Little calf?" he called out.

No one replied.

Curious! he thought. *How curious.*

How was it possible that he couldn't find his friend, the little calf, when all four creatures had been released and the sphinx's riddle had been solved?

All is lost! he thought downheartedly.

He gathered his blue wings and lowered his head. What should he do now? Should he give up? Not a moment passed, however, before he lifted his head and, in a steady voice, said:

"No! No!"

And then a faint spark brightened and began
to grow stronger, livelier and sharper until, like
a little star, it floated among the statues in the gallery.
Every so often, the golden spark would pause and
linger over a statue before changing direction and
continuing on its shimmering path.

Suddenly, with a huge leap, the little spark lit up the shoulders of the Moschophoros.

"Here I am! Here I am!" called out the little calf excitedly.

Hearing the voice of his friend, the little griffin quickly flew to his side. He let out a huge sigh and the two friends embraced lovingly. They were so happy to have found each other.

The power of friendship.

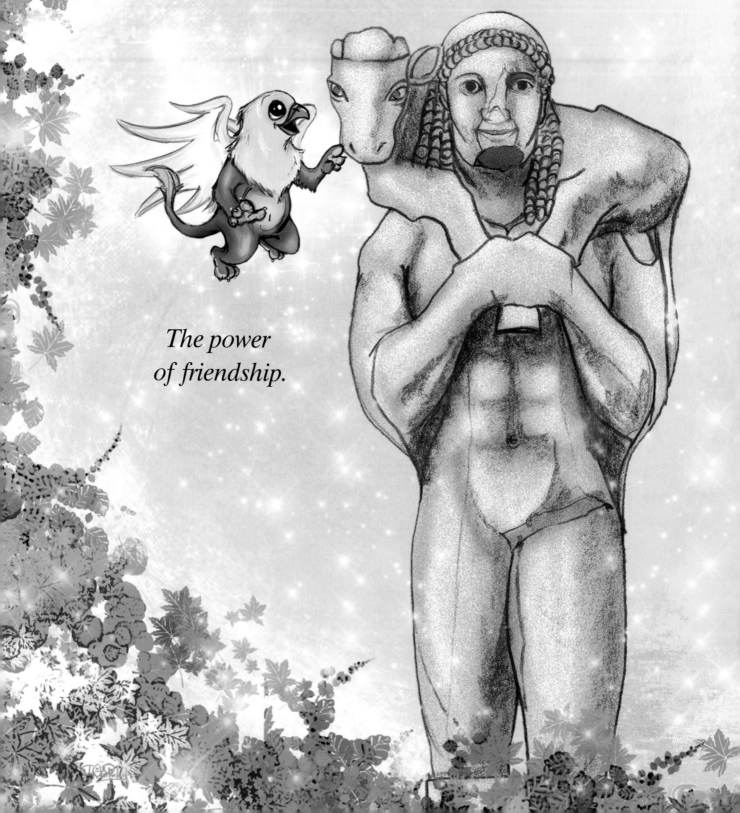

The statues in the gallery had now come alive. They were all talking together, chattering, laughing loudly. In the end, they cheered and applauded both friends with all their might.

And when the excitement died down and the noise slowly faded, the silvery light of the full moon shone through the large glass windows of the museum and wrapped around them tenderly...

And now...

If you want to meet the three-bodied demon, to find out the color of the almond-shaped eyed Kore's chiton, to see the little calf and the horseman's sandal and to meet all the characters from this story... just visit the new Acropolis Museum using these pages as your guide.

Welcome to the new Acropolis Museum!

At the entrance you are welcomed by the two *clay statues of Nike*.

Search a little to your left and find the forehead with the two hazel eyes set into the niche of a pillar. They were an offering from the sanctuary of Asclepius, god of medicine.

Carved in relief on a marble plaque is the *dancer*. The sculptor has depicted her twisting and turning to the rhythm of a fast dance. She has lifted her himation slightly and its deep pleats seem to flutter imperceptibly.

Climbing up the glass staircase, the pediment of the archaic temple to the goddess Athena will draw your attention.

To your left, *Heracles* the hero struggles with *Triton*, the terrible sea monster, which, according to myth, he defeated. To your right, you will see the *three-bodied* demon with his triple body and its three entwined serpent tails. Just imagine how much strength that creature must have possessed!

Now come inside the *Archaic Gallery*.

Here you are welcomed by the *four horses* which archaeologists say pulled a chariot.

Here also are the two *sphinxes* with their female faces.

Very few people can bear their gaze. Of course, to some visitors they are very kind and close their eyes. Hurry now, we must move on!

Go to glass case number 6. There you'll see the *owl*, one of the symbols of Athena, and the *snake made of porous stone* with its wide-open mouth.

All around, you are surrounded by the Korai, beautiful young women. They were votives, gifts to the goddess Athena, and they decorated the holy ground of the Acropolis.

Stay a little and admire the *Peplophoros Kore*. See how happy she looks! Her eyes are literally shining. Her long red hair falls onto her shoulders in waves. They say she portrayed the goddess Demeter and that her long peplos was decorated with animals.

Near her you will find the *horseman* in his multicolored Asian uniform. Isn't it incredible how the blue color of the horse's mane and the red color of his sandal have lasted for so many centuries?

Discover the *Kore* numbered Acr. 682. She depicts
a gentle noblewoman with a beautiful smile, wearing
a rich himation, a wreath in her plaited hair, and earrings.
Then find the *Kore with the almond-shaped eyes*.
Her body is slender, her face serious, her eyes enigmatic.
What could she be thinking? Observe, too, the color of her chiton.

The *Kritios Boy* is also very beautiful and unique. He bends his right
knee slightly and supports his weight with his left leg. With his body
in this position, he appears to be in motion.

Stand with reverence before the *goddess Athena* from the pediment
of the ancient temple depicting the Gigantomachy scene. Look closely at
the aegis with the snakes that she holds in her left hand. In her right hand,
she would have held a spear.

By her side, you can see the *lion's head*. This used to be set on
the corner of the roof and rain water would gush from its open mouth.

Next you will see the votive relief of the *three Charites* (or Graces)
and the little boy. Some archaeologists believe that the piper leading
the dancers represents the god Hermes.

Now go back to glass case number 20 and see *the rooster, the bull, the dog, the bird* and *the lion*. These were all bronze offerings to the temple.

Turning around, exactly before you, you will meet the *Moschophoros*. On his shoulders sits a little calf. It is about to be offered as a sacrifice to the goddess Athena during the Panathenaea religious festival. The youth's name is carved at the base of the statue. Can you read it? (The inscription can be read from right to left.)

Before you leave the museum, take a last look around and imagine what all these statues would have looked like in ancient times, painted in bright vivid colors like blue and red. Just think how beautiful they must have looked on the Holy Rock of the Acropolis as the bright Athens sun shone down on them.

Mania Douka was born in Athens. She studied education in Athens and England. She specialized in museum education at "Atelier des Enfants," Centre Georges Pompidou, in Paris. She worked as a teacher at Arsakeion School, Psychiko College and the Hellenic College of London. She has worked with museums in Athens and Cyprus creating educational programs and printed matter. She has published over 20 books in both Greek and English. Her book *Philip and the Magic Castanets* received the Circle of the Greek Children's Book award (Greek IBBY Section).

Ino Karella was born in Athens. She studied Fine Arts, specializing in Animation at Kent Institute of Art & Design, Experimental Animation at Surrey Institute of Art & Design, completing her training at California Institute of The Arts in Film & Video – Character Animation. With almost two decades of extensive experience, her work consists of a long list of international high-profile projects and collaborations as a production painter, character designer, storyboard artist, animator and illustrator. Her experience and specialization led her to hold the position of Senior Concept Artist at Electronics Arts Los Angeles, developing games such as Medal of Honor, Lord of the Rings, Command & Conquer 3 and Tiberium FPS (Command & Conquer) to name a few. Since 2009 Ino has been freelancing with Greece as her base.